KT-479-185

CLEVER

LOLLIPOP

First published 2003 by Walker Books Ltd
87 Vauxhall Walk, London SE11 5HJ

2 4 6 8 10 9 7 5 3 1

Text © 2003 Foxbusters Ltd
Illustrations © 2003 Jill Barton

The right of Dick King-Smith and Jill Barton to be identified as
author and illustrator respectively of this work has been asserted by them
in accordance with the Copyright, Designs and Patents Act 1988

This book has been typeset in Stempel Schneidler and Gararond

Printed and bound in Great Britain by
Creative Print and Design (Wales), Ebbw Vale

All rights reserved. No part of this book may be reproduced, transmitted
or stored in an information retrieval system in any form or by any means, graphic,
electronic or mechanical, including photocopying, taping and recording,
without prior written permission from the publisher.

British Library Cataloguing in Publication Data:
a catalogue record for this book is
available from the British Library

ISBN 1-84428-627-4

www.walkerbooks.co.uk

CLEVER LOLLIPOP

written by Dick King-Smith

illustrated by Jill Barton

WALKER BOOKS
AND SUBSIDIARIES
LONDON • BOSTON • SYDNEY

CONTENTS

"She ought to have a governess"

CHAPTER ONE

Once upon a time, in a faraway land, a king sat thinking at the big table in the grand banqueting-hall of his great Palace.

His name was King Theophilus, and he was thinking, with pleasure, of the breakfast that was shortly to be brought to him. It was his favourite breakfast – scrambled eggs on fried bread.

In the garden-room, so called because its French windows gave a perfect view of the Royal rose-garden, his wife, Queen Ethelwynne, sat thinking. She was thinking, with pleasure, of the lovely blooms which she could see outside, especially those of a particular rose called Ethelwynne's Beautiful.

Princess Penelope, daughter of the King and the Queen, sat in a room still called the nursery, though she was now too old to need a nursemaid,

thinking, with pleasure, about
her friend Johnny Skinner
and her pig Lollipop.
She spent a good
deal of her time thinking
about one or the other,
perhaps because both of them
– though maybe she did not realize this – had made a
great deal of difference to her and changed her, greatly
for the better.

Princess Penelope had been a selfish, rude and
stubborn child, much spoiled by her father, and a real
pain in the neck to all and sundry. She had demanded
a pet as an eighth birthday present, and not just any
old pet but a pig.

She had chosen one belonging to a very poor boy by
the name of Johnny Skinner. "Lollipop" he called this
pig, and he had taught her to do all manner of clever
tricks. He had even taught her to be house-trained, or

rather palace-trained, for the Princess was determined that Lollipop should be treated just like a pet dog or cat and should sleep at the foot of her bed.

King Theophilus, of course, gave in to everything his daughter wanted. Queen Ethelwynne was a harder nut to crack, but even she was won over when Johnny trained Lollipop to dig over the Royal rose-beds with her snout at his command of "Rootle!" and when he said "Busy!" she would fertilize the roses with her dung which she would deposit at the foot of each bush.

Equally importantly from the Queen's point of view, the pig was perfectly palace-trained, and Johnny Skinner was offered the job of under-gardener and a little cottage to go with it.

Now, as the King was thinking about breakfast and the Queen about roses and the Princess about him, Johnny sat in his little cottage, thinking about his pig.

It's her pig now, he thought, I know that in my mind, but in my heart Lollipop will always be mine. Perhaps

the best way to look at it is that Penelope thinks she's hers and I think she's mine, so she's ours.

Now Johnny was not a boastful sort of boy, but he knew that it was due to him that Princess Penelope had changed from a spoiled brat to a much nicer sort of girl, of whom he'd grown quite fond.

But she should be at school, he thought, learning things. I never went to school, so what little I know I've picked up as I've gone along. For example, I've never learned to read.

Thinking about reading somehow made him think about weeding (something I know how to do, he said to himself with a smile), and he went out into the garden and started work. I wonder, he thought, if Penelope can read properly. She ought to have a governess.

At that moment, Queen Ethelwynne came out through her French windows and walked along a path towards the bed in which Johnny was working. Good boy, she thought, he's doing just what I was going to ask him to do.

"Good morning, Johnny," she said.

Johnny scrambled to his feet.

"Good morning, Your Majesty," he replied.

"When you've finished that," said the Queen, "would you put Lollipop through the rose-beds? They could do with turning over."

"Yes, ma'am," said Johnny.

Lollipop's ideal for roses, he thought, cultivates them with her front end and fertilizes them with her back end. Should I put it like that to Her Majesty? No, perhaps not.

"I've been reading a new book on roses, Johnny," said Queen Ethelwynne. "Would you like to borrow it when I've finished?"

"Kind of you, ma'am," said Johnny, "but I've never been taught to read."

"What!" said the Queen. "How awful for you! Reading is so important."

My chance, thought Johnny. She seems in a good mood. I'll try my luck.

"Princess Penelope is a great reader, I expect, ma'am?" he said.

Ho-hum, thought the Queen, he's very sharp, this boy. I'll see what he has to say.

"In fact," she replied, "Her Royal Highness is not all that interested in books."

"Is that so?" said Johnny. "I've never been to school, of course."

"As a matter of fact," said the Queen, "nor has the Princess."

They looked at one another.

"Are you suggesting something, Johnny?" asked the Queen.

"Yes," said Johnny. "She ought to have a governess."

A few minutes later Queen Ethelwynne burst into the great banqueting-hall, where King Theophilus was still sitting at the big table, eating the last mouthful of a second helping of scrambled eggs on fried bread.

"Theo!" said the Queen.

"Yes, Eth?" said the King, swallowing hastily and mopping his mouth with his napkin.

"I've been thinking. About Penelope. And I've made up my mind."

"Yes, Eth?" said the King.

"She ought to have a governess."

Meanwhile, in the nursery, Lollipop had a problem. Palace-trained she might be, but the morning was drawing on and she had not yet been let out into the garden.

Princess Penelope should, of course, have done this ages ago, but she was in a sort of daydream, thinking about her two friends.

Maybe Johnny still reckons that Lollipop is his, she said to herself, but she's not, she's mine. Perhaps the best way to look at it is that she's ours.

Suddenly she became aware that the pig was standing

close beside her, and then she heard a snuffle and felt a nudge against her leg.

"What's the matter, Lollipop?" asked the Princess, looking into the pig's bright intelligent eyes and seeing someone very like herself looking back.

For answer, Lollipop trotted across to the door of the nursery.

"Oh sorry!" cried the Princess. "You want to go out, is that it?" And in reply the pig gave the one short sharp grunt that meant, as both her owners knew, "Yes".

Quickly Princess Penelope opened the nursery door, and quickly both Princess and pig ran down the corridor that ended in a door which led to the garden.

"Busy!" said the Princess.

Johnny, looking up from his weeding, saw Lollipop rush to the rose-beds.

Once she's made herself comfortable, he thought, I might as well put her straight to work. So he waited until all had been done that needed to be done, and then he called out to the Princess.

"Penelope!" he cried. "Your mother wants Lollipop put through the rose-beds. Can you start her while I'm finishing this weeding?"

"Right-ho, Duke," called Princess Penelope.

Just as Johnny had given up addressing the Princess as "Your Royal Highness" (because she'd asked him to), so now she very often called her friend "Duke" (because King Theophilus had said he would make Johnny one, though actually he'd forgotten to do anything about it).

Now the Princess said to Lollipop "Rootle!" and the pig began to turn over the earth with her snout.

"Thanks, Penelope!" called Johnny. "I'll have finished this weeding in a minute."

Thinking about weeding somehow made him think about reading, and he said, "Lollipop will work on her own. You can go and read a book if you like."

"I don't want to read some old book, Duke," the Princess replied.

You wait, Johnny Skinner said to himself. I've told your mother what I think you need and she'll have told your father and he'll do whatever your mother tells him, and before you can say "Jack Robinson" you'll be being taught to read. By your governess. I wonder what she'll be like?

"Your daughter is very strong-minded"

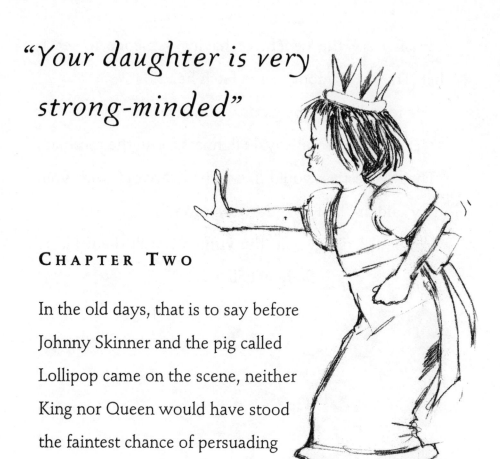

CHAPTER TWO

In the old days, that is to say before
Johnny Skinner and the pig called
Lollipop came on the scene, neither
King nor Queen would have stood
the faintest chance of persuading
the Princess Penelope to have
a governess.

"Will not!" she would
have shouted, and that would have been that.

But now, the King and the Queen said to one another,
their daughter was quite a different child. She would

certainly see the benefit of having someone to teach her. They sent a footman to fetch her.

He found her in the garden, playing with her pig.

"Excuse me, Your Royal Highness," said the footman. "Their Majesties would like to have a word with you, they said. In the Royal drawing-room."

"All right," said the Princess. "Tell them I'll be there in half a tick."

She spent a little time scratching Lollipop's back and telling her how beautiful she was, and then she made her way in through the garden door (that had a special pig-flap fitted in it for Lollipop's use). The pig followed, carefully wiping her trotters on the mat inside as she had been trained to do. Then she walked at heel as Princess Penelope made her way to the drawing-room.

At sight of her the King, who had been sitting down, stood up, and the Queen, who had been standing up, sat down.

"Good morning, darling," they said with one voice.

"Morning Mummy, morning Daddy," the Princess said. "What d'you want?"

"Tell her, Theo," said the Queen.

"No, you tell her, Eth," said the King.

"Tell me what?" asked the Princess.

"Well," said the Queen, smiling sweetly at her daughter, "Daddy and I thought that, now you're such a big girl and so sensible and well behaved, it's time you had someone to help you."

"Help me?" said the Princess. "Help me to do what?"

"To learn things, darling," said the King, beaming broadly at his daughter. "Like reading and writing and arithmetic. We think you'd enjoy having someone to teach you."

"We think," said the Queen, "that you should have a governess. What do you say to that?"

There was a moment's silence, and King and Queen saw that their little daughter was frowning. Oh no, each thought, is it going to be like it used to be? They waited with bated breath for her to shout "Will not!" or to express point-blank refusal of this idea in one way or another.

What they did not expect was that the Princess should make no answer to her mother's question. Instead she turned to the pig, still standing at heel.

"A governess, Lollipop," said the Princess. "Would that be a good idea?"

Lollipop raised her head to look into the girl's eyes. Then she looked at the King. Then she looked at the Queen. Then she gave the short sharp "Yes" grunt.

The Princess turned back to face her anxious parents.

"I'll think about it," she said.

Then she left the drawing-room, the pig following, and made her way back to the garden where Johnny was hard at work.

"You'll never guess," she said to him. "They want me to have a governess."

"Really?" said Johnny.

"Yes," said the Princess. "Just imagine, having to do lessons."

"You're lucky," Johnny said.

"Lucky?"

"Yes. I never had any education but you'll be able to learn all sorts of things. Specially if they get you a really good governess. You're fortunate, Penelope, you are."

"Hm," said the Princess. She thought for a moment. "Tell you what, Johnny," she said. "You could share her with me."

"I don't know," said Johnny, "that your mother and father would like that."

"They will," replied Princess Penelope, "because I'll tell them that I won't have any old governess unless you can have lessons too. That'll fix 'em, won't it, Lollipop?" And the pig grunted "Yes".

Of course the King and the Queen both said "Yes" to the idea of Johnny Skinner having lessons too. To say "No", each realized, would have been most unwise, and so King Theophilus issued a Royal Proclamation, inviting applicants for the post of Governess-to-the-Princess.

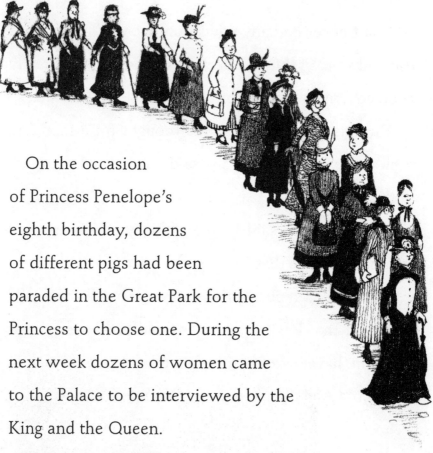

On the occasion
of Princess Penelope's
eighth birthday, dozens
of different pigs had been
paraded in the Great Park for the
Princess to choose one. During the
next week dozens of women came
to the Palace to be interviewed by the
King and the Queen.

There were big ladies and middle-sized
ladies and little ladies, some tall, some short,
some fat, some thin, all very keen to be selected as
Governess-to-the-Princess.

In the end the King and the Queen picked a retired schoolteacher by the name of Miss Gristle. (Or rather, the Queen picked her and the King agreed.)

Miss Gristle was tall and thin with iron-grey hair and a beaky nose, so that she looked like some sort of long-legged bird.

What had been the Princess's nursery was renamed the schoolroom, and in it, at Miss Gristle's request,

were now three desks (a large one for her and two smaller ones for the children) and a blackboard.

There was a supply of chalk for the blackboard, and paper and pencils for the children, and on the walls were a map of the world and a large placard showing all the letters of the alphabet and another with all the numbers up to a hundred.

All was ready for the first morning's schooling.

It did not start too well.

Miss Gristle sat at her large desk awaiting the arrival of her Royal pupil, when the door of the schoolroom opened and in came the Princess and a long-legged boy.

"Good morning, Penelope," said Miss Gristle. And to Johnny she said, "Shut the door, please."

"Half a tick," said the Princess, "we're not all here yet." And then in through the schoolroom door came a short-legged pig.

At sight of Lollipop, Miss Gristle let out a piercing scream.

"It's a pig!"

she cried.

"Full marks," said Penelope. "Well done, you."

"Take it away, take it away. I can't stand pigs!" cried the Governess-to-the-Princess.

"Suit yourself," said Penelope, "but if Lollipop goes, we go too. One out, all out!"

The one that went out, however, was Miss Gristle, her horrified eyes fixed upon the pig as though it had been a woman-eating tiger.

"Silly old thing," said Princess Penelope. "Isn't she, Duke?"

"I must say," replied Johnny Skinner, "I thought you were a bit hard on her. Now she'll probably give in her notice."

"Good," said the Princess.

"But Penelope," said Johnny, "it isn't just you who needs a governess. I do too, remember?"

He turned to Lollipop.

"And you do, don't you, my lady?" And for answer

the pig gave a volley
of those short sharp
"Yes" grunts.

Meanwhile Miss Gristle
had sought out the King
and Queen.

"Your Majesties!" she
cried. "Penelope has
brought a pig into my
schoolroom!"

"Well, it's her pig," said the King.

"But," said the Queen, "it's not necessarily your
schoolroom if you see fit to address our daughter by
her Christian name in that familiar manner. You may
call the boy 'Johnny' and the pig's name is 'Lady
Lollipop', but perhaps you will remember in future to
refer to our daughter as 'Princess Penelope' or, if you
wish, as 'Her Royal Highness'."

Miss Gristle's mouth fell open, but no words came from it.

"And now," said the Queen, "perhaps you would return to your duties." And she swept out of the room.

"Sorry about all this," said the King as he prepared to follow her, "but don't worry about the pig. You'll soon get used to her."

"I shall not, sir," said Miss Gristle in a strangled voice. "I am leaving your employment. Now." And she too swept out.

King Theophilus made his way to the schoolroom, to find his daughter and Johnny Skinner sitting at their desks and Lady Lollipop sitting on the floor.

"Where's old Gristly gone, Daddy?" asked Penelope.

"She has given in her notice."

"Good," said the Princess. "I don't like her and I don't think Johnny does and I'm certain Lady Lollipop doesn't – she kept giving that long deep grunt that means 'No'."

"Your daughter," said the King to his wife later, "is very strong-minded."

"And who does she get that from?" asked the Queen.

"Me?" said the King hopefully.

"If you believe that," said the Queen, "then you'd probably believe that Lollipop might come flying by the window any moment now. Find the child another governess, Theo, and be quick about it."

"He's a sort of magician"

CHAPTER THREE

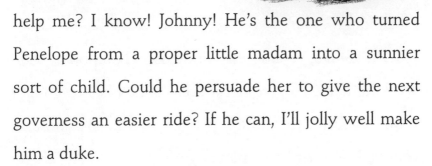

Find another governess, thought the King. It isn't finding one, it's keeping one that's going to be the problem. Suppose Penelope upsets the next one? What should I do? Who could help me? I know! Johnny! He's the one who turned Penelope from a proper little madam into a sunnier sort of child. Could he persuade her to give the next governess an easier ride? If he can, I'll jolly well make him a duke.

"Oh bother!" said King Theophilus out loud. "I'd quite forgotten I'd already promised to make the boy a duke and I haven't done anything about it."

The Princess and the under-gardener were weeding the vegetable patch when a footman came to tell Johnny that the King wanted him.

The weeding was quite easy work because Lady Lollipop was rootling along in front of them, loosening the ground and eating such weeds as she fancied, while being very careful (because Johnny had told her to be) not to disturb the rows of plants of cabbage and cauliflower and Brussels sprouts.

"Your dad wants me," Johnny said to the Princess. "Can you manage on your own for a bit? I don't expect I'll be long."

"OK, Duke," said the Princess. "Lollipop's been working hard, I'll give her a break. She likes to go and rootle about in that rough patch down in the corner. I think there must be some tasty weeds there. Are there, Lollipop?"

And the pig grunted "Yes".

"I'm awfully sorry," said the King when Johnny arrived. "I clean forgot I was going to make you a duke. What would you like to be duke of?"

"I'm not that bothered, sir," said Johnny. "I'm quite happy as I am. Was that what you wanted to see me about?"

"Well, no," said the King. "Actually I wanted to have a chat with you about this governess business. Now Miss Gristle has shoved off because of the pig, I've got to find some other woman to replace her."

"The Princess could have a man as a tutor, sir, couldn't she?" said Johnny. "Preferably someone who likes pigs. Mind you, he'd have to be a bit careful."

"What d'you mean?" said the King.

"Well," said Johnny, grinning, "he'd have to mind his p's and q's and not just call her Penelope like Miss Gristle did."

King Theophilus grinned back. "You don't call her 'Your Royal Highness', Johnny, do you?"

"No, sir. But we're friends. Whoever you get, man or woman, Penelope would have to like the person."

"Look, Johnny," said the King, "d'you think you could find me someone? If you could, I'd jolly well make you a prince."

But before Johnny could answer, the door was flung open and in rushed Princess Penelope.

"Johnny!" she cried. "Come quickly! There's something wrong with Lady Lollipop!" And out she ran again.

"Go on, Johnny," said the King. "Go after her."

In the vegetable patch, Johnny found his pig – Penelope's pig, their pig – lying on her side on top of a squashed row of cabbage plants. Her eyes were closed and she was breathing heavily.

"She went off down to the rough patch," the Princess said, "and after a bit she came back, and then she groaned and collapsed. 'Are you all right?' I asked, and she gave the 'No' grunt. Oh, Duke, whatever's the matter with her?"

Johnny knelt down beside Lollipop. He spoke to her, asking what the matter was, but she only responded with small squeaks of pain.

"I think she must have a fever of some sort," he said.

"Oh, who could help her?" cried Penelope.

"There's only one person," answered Johnny.

"Who?"

"The Conjuror."

"Conjuror? What does that mean?"

"Well, he's a sort of magician. He's got magic powers, they say, and mostly he uses them to cure sick animals."

"Have you met him, Duke?"

"Yes. He's ever such a funny-looking little man."

"I don't care what he looks like," said Penelope, "as long as he can cure Lollipop. Can you find him?"

"Hope so," said Johnny. "You stay with her and talk to her. That will comfort you, won't it, Lollipop?" And this time, at the sound of his voice, the pig feebly grunted "Yes".

For hours, it seemed to the Princess, she sat beside her pig, patting her, stroking her, telling her not to worry, everything would be all right, Johnny would find the Conjuror and he would make her better.

The King and the Queen came out into the gardens to
see what the matter was, and before long there was
a large circle of onlookers standing round the Princess
and Lady Lollipop.

As the news spread, the Lord High Chamberlain
came out and the Comptroller of the Royal Household
and the Master of the Horse and several of the Ladies
of the Bedchamber and a whole lot of footmen.

All of them knew how important the pig was to the happiness of the Princess, and how important the happiness of the Princess was to Their Majesties, and all of them hoped devoutly that Johnny would find the Conjuror.

Then – after ages, it seemed to the Princess, but really after less than an hour – word came that Johnny had been successful in his quest and was on his way, and the King (prompted by the Queen) ordered everyone else to return to their duties.

So that only King Theophilus and Queen Ethelwynne and the Princess Penelope were left to see Johnny Skinner come into the gardens, followed by a very strange figure.

In height, the Conjuror was not much taller than the Princess, so that it seemed as though his beard, which was very long, might trip him up at any moment. He wore strange clothes of many different colours and on his head the oddest sort of tall top hat with no brim.

"May it please Your Majesty," he said to the King in a squeaky voice, "I am Collie Cob, the Conjuror, and I am come to cure Your Majesty's pig."

"It jolly well does please me," said the King, "but she isn't my pig, she's my daughter's. What d'you think is the matter with her?"

The little Conjuror bent his short legs and laid his hands upon the pig's chest, feeling for the beat of her heart. Then he straightened up and addressed Princess Penelope. "Your Royal Highness," he said, "pray what is your pig called?"

"Lady Lollipop," replied the Princess.

"Your Royal Highness," said the Conjuror, "I have to tell you that Lady Lollipop is a very sick pig."

"What's the matter with her?" cried the Princess.

"I think," said the Conjuror, "that she may have eaten some plant or other – deadly nightshade, maybe, or hemlock – that has poisoned her. She has a high fever."

"Oh, please!" cried the Princess. "Can you make her better?"

The Conjuror smiled.

"One thing's certain," he said. "If Collie Cob can't cure her, then nobody can."

"I'll jolly well make you a duke"

CHAPTER FOUR

"How can we help?"
asked the Queen.

"Oh, that is most gracious
of Your Majesty," began the Conjuror.

"This is an emergency," said the Queen, "and we
need to act fast. You can drop all that 'Majesty' business
for now."

At these last words the King looked astonished and Johnny Skinner, catching the Princess's eye, winked at her with one of his own.

"Well," said the Conjuror to the Queen, "I shall need boiling water. Could you put the kettle on?"

"What can I do?" asked the King.

"I shall want a big jug and a large bowl," said Collie Cob, and off went the King and Queen to the Royal kitchens.

"What about us?" asked the Princess and Johnny with one voice.

"You two," said the Conjuror, "can be collecting all that I shall need to make up a potion."

"A magic potion?" asked the Princess.

The Conjuror smiled.

"We shall see," he replied. "Now, here are the things I shall want. The first and most important, Johnny – and I'm asking you to find it because you're a gardener – is a big bunch of feverfew."

"What's that, Mr Cob?" asked Johnny.

"This is an emergency," said the Conjuror, "and we need to act fast. You can drop all that 'Mr Cob' business for now." And he grinned, his blue eyes twinkling. "Feverfew, Johnny, is a plant of the daisy family, related to camomile and very effective in reducing fever. I just happened to notice a patch of it by the gate we came in through. And while you're about it, get me some spinach leaves and a head of broccoli and a big dandelion. Quick as you can!"

"What about me?" asked Princess Penelope.

"I need two eggs," said the Conjuror. "One brown, one white, and an eggcupful of mustard lightly salted, and the juice of a lemon. Break the eggs into a bowl and stir the rest in. Away you go!"

Alone with Lollipop, whose breathing was still loud and laboured, the Conjuror lifted one of her big ears and spoke softly into it. Had anyone heard his words, they would not have understood them, for they were in a strange tongue, but the pig's eyelids fluttered and she gave one tiny grunt that might have been a "Yes".

Once everyone was back with what the Conjuror had ordered, he set about concocting his potion.

Into a large bowl that King Theophilus had brought, he tipped the mixture that Princess Penelope had made up. Then he brought out from a bag that he carried a great pair of scissors and a wooden ladle. He chopped very small the dandelion, the broccoli, the spinach and

the big bunch of feverfew that Johnny Skinner had provided, and added them to the mix. Lastly, he took from Queen Ethelwynne the kettle of boiling water and poured it in, and with the wooden ladle he stirred and stirred and stirred the thick green compound.

"Now," he said, "we'll wait for it to cool a bit."

"But how are you going to give it to her?" asked the Princess. "She can't get up, so how will she drink it?"

For answer the Conjuror took from his bag a little funnel and a length of rubber tubing. He fitted them together, slipped the end into Lollipop's mouth and eased it in until he was satisfied that it was down her throat.

Then, after making sure that the mixture was cool enough, he lifted the large bowl (with the King's help, for it was heavy) and between them they tipped it, to pour its contents slowly into the big jug, and thence into the funnel and thus into the tubing and thus into the pig, until the bowl was empty.

Then the Conjuror gently withdrew the length of tubing.

At first it did not seem to the watchers that the potion had had any effect. Still Lady Lollipop lay flat on her side, her eyes closed. Still they heard that harsh painful breathing. Penelope and Johnny both crossed their fingers. The King and Queen held hands tightly.

But then, gradually, to the amazement of the Royal Family and Johnny, the pig's breathing began to quieten. Then her eyelids started to flutter. Then the one eye that they could see slowly opened. Lastly – and loudly – Lady Lollipop let out the most enormous belch.

"She'll be right as rain now," said the Conjuror. "Come on, Lady Lollipop, up you get!"

And up she got!

"Oh, Lollipop!" cried the Princess. "Are you all right, my dear?"

At which the pig gave a loud and definite "Yes" grunt, shook herself and looked around with bright eyes at each person in turn. She looked particularly gratefully at the short figure of Collie Cob, the Conjuror, whose hand the King was now heartily shaking.

"Marvellous!" said King Theophilus. "You're a wizard, Mr Cob! I'll jolly well make you a duke!"

Johnny Skinner spoke softly in the Conjuror's ear.

"I shouldn't rely on it, if I were you," he said.

"Bird droppings and slug slime and mashed mouse manure"

CHAPTER FIVE

"Well, anyway," said the King, "you must let us pay you for your services. You have saved Lollipop's life. What do we owe you?"

"Oh, bless you, sir, that's all right," said the Conjuror. "I'm glad to have been of service. To have lost such a fine young pig would have been a tragedy. She's going to grow into a beautiful sow. I can just see her with a litter of lovely little piglets."

At this the King smiled broadly, Johnny grinned with delight, and the Princess Penelope jumped up and down in excitement. Even the pig let out a string of quick high-pitched grunts to show her pleasure at the Conjuror's forecast.

Only the Queen looked doubtful. Fond as she was by now of her daughter's pet, she recoiled at the thought of nine or ten miniature Lollipops scampering around in the Palace.

She picked up the kettle.

"Come and have a cup of tea," she said, and off she marched, the Conjuror following.

The King picked up the big jug and the large bowl and the smaller bowl in which Penelope had brought the mixture for the potion.

"Coming?" he said to the two children.

"No, Daddy," said the Princess. "I'm going to stay with Lollipop. You go if you want, Johnny."

"No," said Johnny, "I'll stay with you."

Once King and Queen and Conjuror were all seated round the Royal dining-table drinking tea, King Theophilus tried once more to offer payment for the treatment of the pig, but the Conjuror was adamant.

"No, sir," he said, "thanking you kindly. I treat all kinds of animals for all kinds of people but I never charge for my services, for most of those who seek my help are poor folk."

"We're not," said the Queen.

"No, ma'am, but I never take money from anyone. The most I accept, from those that can afford it, is payment in kind – a couple of pounds of potatoes perhaps or a bundle of firewood or a dozen eggs."

"How are we to thank you then?" asked the Queen.

What a strange little man he is, she thought, with his squeaky voice and his many-coloured clothes and his funny hat.

"Well, ma'am," said the Conjuror, "there is one favour that Your Majesties could grant me, and that is to let me come back now and again, to see that Lollipop is all right and to meet again with your daughter and the boy Johnny and to admire once more that beautiful garden of roses – my favourite flowers – that we passed just now."

What a lovely little man he is,
thought the Queen.

"How do you grow such wonderful blooms, may I ask?" said the Conjuror. "What is the secret of your success?"

"Pig dung," said the Queen.

"First class!" squeaked the Conjuror. "Some rose-growers prefer horse dung, but I think pig is the best. Whilst we're on the subject, I notice that your bushes suffer from that scourge of rose-growers – black spot."

"They do, they do," said the Queen. "I don't know what to do about it and nor does Johnny. It worries us no end."

"Worry no more," said the Conjuror.

"Why? Can you cure it?"

"I can, ma'am. If you will allow me I will treat the affected leaves with a special dressing of my own invention, a mixture of bird droppings and slug slime and mashed mouse manure."

"Then by all means," cried the Queen, "come back to my rose-garden as soon as you can, Mr Cob, and come as often as you can to visit us and the children!"

"And the pig," added the King.

What a clever little chap he is, he thought.

"What a knowledgeable fellow you are, to be sure," he said. "First you cure the pig and now you're going to put my wife's roses to rights. What favour, I wonder, will you do us next?"

"It depends, sir," said the Conjuror. "Has Your Majesty any other problem at the present time?"

"Yes!" said the King. "Come to think of it, I jolly well have. We need a governess." And he told the Conjuror all about the newly departed Miss Gristle.

"You don't know of any woman suitable for the job, I suppose?" he asked.

For a moment the little Conjuror did not answer but looked reflectively at King Theophilus and Queen Ethelwynne.

What a nice couple they are,
    he thought.

I dare say I could teach the two children quite a lot. It'd be fun to try.

"Does it have to be a woman?" he asked.

Funny, thought the King, that's just what Johnny said.

"No," he replied, "it could be a man. We need someone to teach the Princess reading and writing and arithmetic and all that sort of stuff."

"And to teach the boy too," said the Queen.

"And the pig," said the King. "She's pretty bright."

"Then, sir," said the Conjuror, "I think I know of a man who would like to try his hand at that job."

"You do?" cried the King and Queen together.

"Yes."

"Who?" they said.

"Me," replied Collie Cob, the Conjuror.

"When can you start?" they cried.

"How would you like to be Penny?"

CHAPTER SIX

In fact it was a week before the new tutor entered the schoolroom.

First, there were several sick animals that the Conjuror had to treat –

a horse with
the staggers,

a cow with bloat,

some sheep
with swayback

and a goat with garget –

and, secondly, he needed to make up that mixture of bird droppings and slug slime and mashed mouse manure, to rid the Queen's roses of black spot.

But at last the day came when the Conjuror and the Princess and Johnny Skinner and Lady Lollipop all met within the Palace schoolroom.

The Princess Penelope was the first to speak.

"Please," she said, "what are we to call you?"

"Well," said the Conjuror, "my name, as you know, is Collie Cob. You could call me Mr Cob, I suppose, but that doesn't sound friendly enough to me, so why don't you just call me 'Collie'?"

Johnny grinned and the pig gave a grunt that definitely meant "I agree" and Penelope said, "OK, Collie. Thanks."

"And what, pray," said the Conjuror, "would you like me to call you?"

The Princess smiled.

"Just Penelope," she said.

"Very well," said the Conjuror. "Though I've just had

a thought. There's a sort of plant that I often use in making my potions. It's a kind of mint and its name is pennyroyal. You're royal, so how would you like to be Penny?"

"Suits me, Collie."

"Now then," said the Conjuror, "this morning we're going to think about numbers. Tell me, Penny, how many of us are there in this schoolroom?"

"Four," said the Princess.

"How many humans, Johnny?"

"Three."

"How many females, Penny?"

"Two."

"How many grown-ups, Johnny?"

"One."

The Conjuror turned to Lady Lollipop.

"How many pigs?" he asked her, and the answer was one sharp grunt.

"I don't know what you two think," said Collie Cob,

"but I don't much like this old schoolroom, specially when the sun is shining. How about doing lessons outside?"

"Great!" said Penelope and Johnny and "Grunt!" said Lollipop.

So they all three went out into the garden with the Conjuror.

How can he teach us out here, the children were thinking, without all that stuff Miss Gristle had in the schoolroom?

But then Collie said, "Right. Off we go!"

"Where are we going?" they asked.

"For a walk."

"Where to?"

"Round the town."

"Why?"

"We're going to do some reading," Collie said. "There'll be signs to read, wherever we go, and I can teach you what they say."

And sure enough, even while they were still in the Palace grounds, they came across lots of notices saying,

KEEP OFF THE GRASS

and

PRIVATE
NO ENTRY

and

TRESPASSERS WILL
BE PROSECUTED

And once they were in the town, there were things to read everywhere: the names of streets, the names of shopkeepers, and the names of things for sale in the shops, like, for instance, in the greengrocer's – **APPLES, ORANGES, BANANAS, TOMATOES, CABBAGES, CARROTS,** on and on.

And there were lots of numbers too – the numbers on price-tags, the numbers of houses – so that by the end of that first morning, Penelope and Johnny had done a lot of work with words and figures.

As for Lady Lollipop, she had had a lovely time in the greengrocer's, for the shopkeeper was only too eager to offer the Princess's pet pig a lot of lovely fruit and vegetables.

"The facts I'm going to learn today"

CHAPTER SEVEN

Never was there such a
tutor as Collie Cob, the
Conjuror. Admittedly he
was teaching two very
keen pupils – Johnny
Skinner revelling in
learning how to read
and to write, and the Princess, quick and
bright, who was learning to enjoy reading stories and
indeed to begin writing some of her own making, in
a clear bold hand.

The pair of them were not being taught every day, for
the Conjuror was sometimes called upon to treat a sick

animal, but then they did not need as many lessons as ordinary children would have done, because most of the many things the Conjuror taught them seemed to stick.

Once told a fact, they seldom forgot it.

"It's magic, Duke, isn't it?" said the Princess to her friend after they'd been having lessons for a couple of weeks.

"It must be, Penny," Johnny replied (he had taken to calling her that too now). "It's all to do with that little rhyme that Collie taught us."

For before a day's lessons – whether in reading or writing or maths or history or geography or science – the Princess and Johnny would solemnly chant together:

"The facts I'm going to learn today
Will have a job to go away.
Most will remain inside my brain.
I shan't need to be told again."

And the magic worked!

The King and Queen were amazed at the things the children knew, which they didn't.

The Princess Penelope specially enjoyed examining her parents.

"Daddy," she said to the King. "Do you know the date of the spring equinox?"

"Er, no," said King Theophilus. (What's an equinox? he thought.)

"Twenty-first of March," said his daughter. "And the autumn equinox?"

"Um, er, twenty-first of September?" said the King.

"No, Daddy, no, it's the twenty-third of September."

"I should have thought you'd have known that, Theo," said the Queen sniffily.

"You did, Mummy, did you?" Penelope asked.

"Any fool would know that," replied Queen
Ethelwynne.

"In that case, Mummy," said Penelope, "you obviously
know what an equinox is?"

The Queen hesitated.

"Oh come on, Eth," said the King. "Any fool would
know that."

"An equinox," said the Princess Penelope, "is either
of the two points at which the ecliptic intersects the
celestial equator. OK, Mummy? OK, Daddy?"

As for Johnny Skinner, Collie Cob, realizing the boy's interest in gardening, slipped in some lessons in botany and biology which resulted, amongst other things, in great improvements to the Queen's roses (free now of black spot) and made Her Majesty even more delighted with her under-gardener.

So the weeks and months passed, and the Conjuror's two pupils gained more and more knowledge of more and more things.

As for Lollipop, she seemed to grow wiser and wiser.

One day when the children were playing and the pig and her tutor were resting on the Royal grass (not keeping off it at all), the Conjuror said to her, in her own language, "You're a clever girl, Lollipop, aren't you?"

In answer there came a very loud "Yes" grunt.

"A moly is a magic herb"

CHAPTER EIGHT

Of course, there are lots of things that humans can do which pigs can't.

But, apart from being a very intelligent pig, Lollipop had two advantages over the children, over the King and Queen, even over Collie Cob. She had a very acute sense of smell, and she had a snout specially designed for rootling in the ground.

By chance the day came when she needed both these gifts.

For some time King Theophilus had been worried about his increasing weight, for he had become a great deal more tubby.

One day the Queen had said to him, "Honestly, Theo, you're getting as fat as a pig!"

The remark was light-hearted, but the more the King thought about it, the more he became determined to go on a diet.

At breakfast, his usual ration of two helpings of scrambled eggs on fried bread became one helping only.

Then he told them not to bother with the fried bread.

Then he said he'd just have one boiled egg.

By rights he should have become hungrier as he ate less. But instead, the less he ate, the less hungry he felt. At last one morning – and this worried the Queen greatly – he said he didn't feel like any breakfast at all, but just sat at the table, looking pale (and much thinner).

Queen Ethelwynne called in all sorts of different
doctors, who examined the King and scratched their

heads and finally confessed that they did not have a clue how to restore the King's appetite.

Leaving her husband sitting gloomily at the breakfast table, the Queen went out into the garden and there found Johnny Skinner hard at work, though it was drizzling with rain.

"Oh, Johnny!" she cried. "His Majesty is most unwell and none of the doctors know why. If he doesn't start to eat properly again soon, he'll just fade away. What shall I do?"

Just then Princess Penelope stuck her head out of the schoolroom window. "Johnny!" she shouted. "Collie says lessons in here this morning because of the rain."

"Coming!" called Johnny. And to the Queen he said, "It sounds to me, Your Majesty, as though the King needs a touch of magic to make him better."

"Magic?" said the Queen. "You mean...?" And she pointed up to the schoolroom window.

Johnny nodded.

Lessons that morning consisted of reading, because Collie Cob, the Conjuror, was called away by the Queen to examine the King, leaving the Princess with her nose in a book about astronomy (on which she was very keen), and Johnny with his nose in a book entitled *The Values of Various Kinds of Manure in Garden Fertilization* (something that interested him greatly).

Lollipop snoozed in an armchair.

Both the children shut their books with a snap when the Conjuror came back into the schoolroom.

"Oh, Collie!" cried Penelope. "Whatever's the matter with Daddy, do you know?"

"He's lost his appetite," said the Conjuror. He patted Lollipop's head. "That's something pigs don't usually do," he said, smiling.

"Can you cure him?" the children said.

"With a little help from someone," he replied. "Now then, Penny and Johnny, you've read long enough. Time you had a break. Off you go and play."

When they had gone, the Conjuror called Lollipop out of her chair and invited her to sit in front of the blackboard. Then he took a piece of chalk and drew upon it what seemed to be a picture of a plant of some kind, an odd-looking plant with a feathery top and – below a line which he drew across the board – a strange bulbous root, not round or oval like a potato, for example, but long and curved, the shape of a banana.

Then he began to speak to Lollipop in pig language, a curious mixture of snuffles and snorts and squeaks.

"Now see these leaves," he said to her, pointing above the chalk line on the blackboard, "and this root" – pointing below. "This, Lollipop, is a picture of a moly. A moly is a magic herb, a species of wild onion, and I am going to take you out in the woods to see if you can find one for me. I cannot show you exactly what it smells like because I haven't got one to show you. But if you can rootle up anything that smells oniony and you find that its root is shaped like a banana, then that's a moly. And only a moly can cure the King."

That afternoon Collie Cob asked the children if they would like a walk in the woods.

"It's a lovely day," he said to them, "and Lady Lollipop will enjoy a bit of exercise. Who knows, she might find something exciting."

"What d'you mean?" asked the Princess.

"Like what?" asked Johnny.

"Oh, I don't know," said the Conjuror, dressed, as always, in his curious many-coloured clothes and wearing his tall brimless top hat.

He smiled.

"Pigs are good at finding things. You never can tell what she might turn up."

Once in the woods the two children, at the Conjuror's suggestion, ran off among the trees to play hide-and-seek.

"It's the same game for you, Lollipop," the Conjuror said. "The moly's hiding and you're seeking. Does this feel like a good sort of place to you?" And the pig gave the "Yes" grunt.

For quite a while she snuffled around, occasionally rootling up plants with her snout, but not finding what she'd been told to find.

Collie was about to lead her on to a different part of the woods when suddenly he heard Lollipop give a loud excited squeal as she came across an odd-looking plant with a feathery top.

Quickly she dug around it with her strong (and by now very dirty) snout, and hoicked it up out of the ground, root and all, a root that was the shape of a banana.

She picked up the whole plant and laid it carefully at the feet of the Conjuror.

"You," said he, "are a very clever pig," and he called loudly, "Penny! Johnny!" and when they came running, he picked up the plant and waved it at them.

"Whatever's that?" asked the Princess.

And Johnny, the gardener, said, "What a strange-looking root it's got. What is it?"

"This," said Collie Cob, "is a magic plant called a moly, which clever Lollipop has found for us. From its root I can make a preparation that will restore the appetite of someone who's lost his."

"Dad!" cried Princess Penelope.

The Conjuror nodded.

"Come on," he said. "We must hurry back to the Palace. There's no time to be lost, for only a moly can save your father's life."

"Anything to stop you all nagging me"

CHAPTER NINE

The four of them made their way out of the woods, the Conjuror carrying the moly, Penny and Johnny on either side of him, Lollipop bringing up the rear and stopping every now and again to rootle up something that looked to her good to eat and then galloping after them to catch up.

"Daddy hasn't got to eat all of that funny root, has he?" the Princess asked.

"No, he hasn't," replied Collie. "He wouldn't anyway because he's lost his appetite for any sort of food. But he still has to drink – everybody must have liquid to stay alive."

"So you're going to make the moly into a drink, are you?" Johnny asked.

"Yes," said the Conjuror. "When I get it home, I'll chop the root up small and pound the bits into a nice squishy mess, and then boil them. Then I'll drain off all the liquid – magic liquid – and give it to the King to drink."

Later that day, when the Conjuror came back to the Palace, the children and the pig could see that he was carrying a flask full of a thin golden fluid.

"This is the stuff," he said to the Princess, "to bring your father's appetite back."

"Can I have a swig of it first?" Penelope said.

"No!" said Collie Cob. "You certainly cannot, you stupid girl."

These words turned Princess Penelope back into the spoiled child she had once been. She stamped her foot and shouted at the Conjuror, "How dare you call me a stupid girl! Have you forgotten that I am a princess?"

Behind her back Johnny Skinner put a hand over his mouth to hide a broad grin.

"No, I have not forgotten," said Collie Cob, "and kindly don't shout at me like that, Penny. I can tell you that if you were to drink some of this stuff, it would give you such a raging appetite that you'd eat and eat until you blew up like a balloon. You'd end up the

fattest princess in the whole wide world."

"And we don't want that, do we, Lollipop?" said Johnny, and the pig gave a loud "No" grunt.

"Come on," said the Conjuror. "We'll all go and watch the King take his medicine."

They found King Theophilus sitting once more at the big table in the grand banqueting-hall, where Queen Ethelwynne was trying to tempt him with a number of savoury dishes.

"Try a little of this, Theo," she was saying. "Just a little, to please me. Or some of this ... or this ... or a taste of this."

But the King only said sadly, "I'm not hungry, Eth. I don't want anything to eat."

The Conjuror came forward, flask in one hand, a glass in the other.

"Excuse me," he said to the pale-faced King, "but I have a drink here which I think Your Majesty might find refreshing."

He filled the glass with the thin golden fluid.

"Can I persuade you to try a little sip?" he said.

"No," said the King.

"Oh do, Theo, please!" cried the Queen.

"Please drink it, Daddy," cried the Princess.

"It'll do you good, sir," said Johnny.

The Conjuror held out the glass.

"Just try it," he said.

"Oh, all right, if I must," growled the King. "Anything

to stop you all nagging me."
And he took the glass and
looked at it and sniffed it,
while Lollipop gave a little
volley of "Yes" grunts.

Then he took a sip of the
magic draught made from
the moly.

Immediately, they could all see, his dull eyes
brightened and a little colour came back into his grey
cheeks.

Then he took several big gulps.

Then he drained the glass.

As they all watched,
King Theophilus rose
to his feet, looking
around him somewhat
dazedly, as though
waking from a bad dream.

Then he shouted at the top of his voice, **"Breakfast! I want my breakfast!"**

"But Theo," said Queen Ethelwynne, "it's teatime."

"He wants to break his fast," said the Conjuror quietly to the Queen.

So she said to her husband, "What would you like?"

"Scrambled eggs!" the King shouted. "A double helping of scrambled eggs! With three rounds of fried bread! And be quick about it, I'm starving!"

Back in the schoolroom, the Princess said to the Conjuror, "Thank you, Collie. Thank you so much for bringing Daddy's appetite back – for saving his life in fact. And I'm sorry I shouted at you. It was very rude of me."

"Good for you," said Johnny under his breath.

"That's all right, Penny," said the Conjuror. "Anyway, I couldn't have cured your father without the magic moly and I couldn't have found that without Lollipop's help. Now then, why don't you both go and see how the King's getting on with his meal?"

In fact, when they reached the banqueting-hall, the King was on his third helping of scrambled eggs and his fourth bit of fried bread, and waiting on the table beside him was another of his favourite dishes: cold rice pudding with lashings of strawberry jam.

Left alone with Lollipop, Collie Cob had a word in her great ear.

"I rather think," he said, "that King Theophilus is making a pig of himself."

"Good old Lady Lollipop"

CHAPTER TEN

Thanks to the moly,
a whole lot of things
now changed for
King Theophilus.

First, of course,
his appetite was
restored, and how! Happily he ate, all day long, and as
a result put on so much weight that Queen Ethelwynne
decided he must take some exercise.

"Go for a walk," she said.

"By myself?" said the King.

"Well, I've got too much to do in the Palace and in the
gardens, and Penelope and Johnny have their lessons
with the Conjuror."

"The pig's not doing anything," said the King.

"All right then, take her with you on your walks. Exercise won't do her any harm."

So the second new thing that happened was that every morning, once he had digested a very big breakfast, the King would set out from the Palace with Lady Lollipop beside him. She did not need a collar and lead as a dog would have done, but walked to heel at the King's side and did everything he told her, like "Stop!" (when he wanted to talk to a passer-by) or "Sit!" (when he needed a breather).

The third thing that happened was that the King found himself becoming extremely fond of his daughter's pet. He remembered how small and skinny she had been when first they'd set eyes on her. Now she was a fine strong pig. She was good company on his walks and he talked to her a good deal as they went along, telling her what a good and beautiful pig she was, and how grateful to her he was for finding (as the Conjuror had told him) the moly.

"I'd like to do something for you in return," said the King. "Is there something you specially want?" And in reply Lollipop let out a fusillade of excited noises (which of course meant nothing to the King).

One day he said to the Conjuror, "Look here, Cob, I'd very much like your advice. I think you know that I take Lollipop for regular walks now – my wife's got a bee in her bonnet about me needing exercise – and the pig talks to me a good deal, but of course I can't understand pig language." King Theophilus laughed heartily. "Just imagine, if one could!" he said.

"Just imagine," said the Conjuror.

"You see," said the King, "I'm curious to know what the animal wants, because I'm fairly sure there's something on her mind. You couldn't help, I suppose, Cob, could you?"

"It's possible," said the Conjuror. "I'll have a word with her."

"Have a word with her!" laughed the King. "You'd have to speak her own language to do that!"

"Just so," said the Conjuror.

"Anyway," said the King, "see if you can work out what it is that Lollipop wants. I'd like to do something for her. Fancy her finding that ... what's it called?"

"Moly."

"Yes, that's it. Good old Lady Lollipop! I'll jolly well make her a duchess," said the King.

Next morning, a lovely sunny morning, they were having lessons in the garden.

"Your father," said Collie Cob to the Princess, "says he's going to make Lady Lollipop a duchess."

"Pigs might fly!" said the Princess scornfully. "Daddy's always saying things like that."

She turned to Johnny.

"Isn't he, Duke?" she said.

Johnny smiled.

"Don't get excited," she said to the Conjuror, "if he offers to make you Sir Collie Cob. He always forgets."

"Well," said the Conjuror, "luckily you two will never forget any of the things that I have taught you. Like, for instance, Gondwanaland. What was Gondwanaland, Penny?"

"A supercontinent," replied the Princess, "which is

believed to have existed more than two hundred million years ago. It probably consisted of South America, Africa, Australia, Antarctica and India."

"Quite right," said the Conjuror. "Now, one for you, Johnny. What is a numbat?"

"It's a rat-sized marsupial," said Johnny, "with white stripes across its back and a long tail, and it feeds on ants and termites with its sticky tongue."

"And how are numbats different from all other marsupials?" Collie asked.

"They don't have a pouch."

"Good," said the Conjuror. "And here's one for both of you. How far is Earth from the sun?"

And with one voice they replied, "Ninety-three million miles!"

"Right," said the Conjuror. "Have a break now. Run to the bottom of the garden and back." And as they dashed off, he said to Lady Lollipop, "Stay here with me a minute."

He looked into those bright eyes, fringed with long white lashes and filled with intelligence, and saw someone not so very different from himself looking back at him.

The pig in her turn looked up at the funny little man dressed in many-coloured clothes and wearing that odd brimless top hat, and made the kind of noise that meant, "What's up, then?"

"Now then, Lollipop," said the Conjuror, "the King tells me that he thinks there's something on your mind. Nothing wrong with you, is there? You're not feeling ill again?"

In reply came that deep long-drawn-out "No" grunt.

"Well, what is it that you want?"

The children arrived back from their race – Johnny won, he had longer legs – in time to hear Lollipop's answer, a babble of grunts and squeaks and snorts and snuffles.

"She's trying to tell us something," said the Princess. "I wish I knew what she wants."

"I think I can guess," said Johnny. "My Lollipop" – he turned to smile at Penny – "*our* Lollipop, is a healthy young female, nearly full-grown now."

Johnny Skinner and Penelope looked at Collie Cob and then they looked at one another.

"Of course!" they said with one voice. "She wants babies!"

"Dark and handsome"

CHAPTER ELEVEN

The Conjuror thought carefully about what the pig wanted. The Princess would be delighted at the idea and so would Johnny, and the King too, now that he'd become so fond of Lollipop. The Queen though, she might not be all that keen.

Well, said Collie Cob to himself, we must make some changes.

"Penny," he said to the Princess, "does Lollipop still
sleep on your bed?"

"Yes."

"Plenty of room for
her, is there?"

"Well..."

"Still get up the stairs
quite easily, can she?"

"Well..."

"She doesn't disturb you

at nights, by snoring or making any other noises?"

"Well, she..."

"Don't you think," said the Conjuror, "that it's time she had a room of her own?"

"A bedroom, you mean?"

"Yes. Downstairs. Close to the pig-flap."

"That reminds me," said the Princess. "She's getting too big for that pig-flap. The other day she got stuck in it and Johnny and I had to get a footman to help us push her through."

"That's no problem," said the Conjuror. "We'll get the Royal carpenters to make a larger one. Now then, about a room for her – there's that nice one right next to the schoolroom. It doesn't seem to be used for anything much."

"I'll ask Mummy if I can have it for Lollipop," the Princess said.

"Good," said the Conjuror. "Or perhaps, better still, tell Mummy you want it for Lollipop."

In fact Queen Ethelwynne was quite pleased with the idea. Fond as she had become of Lollipop because of all the good she did in the rose-garden, cultivating the soil with her snout and manuring it at the other end, she had never been all that keen on the pig walking over her priceless carpets or up the stairs, nor on her sleeping in Penelope's bedroom.

So she gave orders for the nice room next door to the schoolroom to be cleared of its furniture and (at the Princess's suggestion) for its carpet to be covered in a good thick layer of horse-blankets from the Royal Mews, to make a really comfortable bed.

Not until Lollipop was settled into her new quarters and a new, much larger, pig-flap had been fitted, did the Conjuror take King Theophilus into his confidence.

"You remember," he said to the King, "you wanted me to find out what was on the pig's mind?"

No, thought the King.

"Yes," he said.

"Well, we've found out what she wants!" cried Johnny and the Princess together.

"What does she want then?"

"Babies."

"Babies!" cried the King. "Oh I say, what fun, Cob!"

"What about your wife, sir?"

"Well, we needn't say anything to her, need we? Let's make it a surprise."

"If you like."

"Can you fix it, Cob?" said the King. "Can you arrange it all? I mean, do you know someone who keeps a ... what do you call a ... father pig?"

"A boar."

"Yes, that's it."

"Yes, I do."

"If you can fix it," said the King excitedly, "I'll jolly well make you a knight! Sir Collie Cob! How does that sound?"

Awful, thought the Conjuror.

"Very nice," he said.

Now amongst all the many things that the Conjuror knew was the fact that it takes a sow three months, three weeks and three days to have babies.

In the schoolroom he steered the conversation round to birthdays.

"When's yours, Johnny?" he asked.

"December the ninth," said Johnny.

"And yours, Penny?"

"June the twenty-third."

Quickly the Conjuror did a sum in his head. It might work out just right, he thought. It's the middle of February now, so if I take Lollipop to the boar towards the end of the month, then the piglets might be born round about Penny's birthday. *On* Penny's birthday, he said to himself. With a bit of luck. Or magic.

"When's yours, Collie?" the Princess asked.

"April the first."

So, nearly two weeks later, it was not King Theophilus who took Lady Lollipop for her daily walk. It was Collie Cob. He had told her, of course, what he had planned for her and asked her if she thought it was a good idea, and she had replied that it was a very good idea indeed, and, in a salvo of excited snorts and snuffles, asked, "What's he like, this boar?"

"Dark and handsome," said the Conjuror.

"Oh, Collie, you fixed it!"

CHAPTER TWELVE

If you're eagerly waiting for something to happen, time can pass very slowly.

Not only the King but also Johnny Skinner (who had been told but sworn to secrecy) knew that Lollipop was, in due course, to become a mother. But that due course – of three months, three weeks and three days – seemed an awful long time.

Lollipop didn't seem worried by the wait. She enjoyed her food and her daily exercise with the King, and slept like a log in her new bedroom, from which, when she needed to, it was easy to pop out into the garden through the new very large pig-flap.

For the Queen and the Princess Penelope, time passed at its usual rate for neither was expecting anything unusual to happen. The Queen was happy in her garden and Penelope was happy having lessons with the Conjuror and being taught so many interesting facts, none of which, once learned, was ever forgotten.

She still rather liked to show off her new-found knowledge to her parents.

"Mummy," she might say to the Queen, "do you know what is the national language of India?"

"Indian, I suppose," replied her mother.

"No, it's Hindi. A hundred and eighty million Indians speak it."

"Oh," said the Queen.

Or, "Daddy," she might say to the King, "d'you know what a moa is?"

"Thing you cut the lawn with," said the King.

"No, not M–O–W–E–R. M–O–A."

"Oh. No. Haven't a clue."

"It's an extinct flightless bird that used to live in New Zealand. It had a little head and a long neck and it could run very fast."

"Proper clever clogs you are," said the King one day. "But I bet I know something that you don't."

"What?"

"Can't tell you. It's a secret."

"Oh go on, Daddy!"

"You'll find out before you're much older," said the King.

"It's my birthday soon," said his daughter. "Just in case you forget. Has this secret got anything to do with that?"

The King winked at her, but he wouldn't say another word.

The Princess consulted Johnny.

"Duke," she said. "Daddy's on about some secret,

something to do with my birthday, I think. D'you know anything about it?"

"Yes."

"What is it?"

"It's a secret."

The Princess's face darkened and she frowned furiously and stamped her foot, which made Johnny smile, remembering what she used to be like.

"What are you grinning at, Duke?" she said angrily.

"Patience, Penny," said Johnny.

"Patience is a virtue,
Virtue is a grace,
Grace is a little girl
Who wouldn't wash her face."

Before she went to bed that night, the Princess went into Lollipop's new quarters to give her her supper. She stood watching as the pig golloped down a great deal of food.

"You're certainly very hungry these days, Lady Lollipop," she said, "and you seem to be getting fatter too." In reply the pig made a lot of loud snorty snuffly squeaky noises.

"I wish I could understand what you're saying," sighed the Princess. "Still, you look pretty happy. Are you happy?" And in reply came half a dozen loud clear "Yes" grunts.

Of course, Lady Lollipop's original owner knew why she was eating so heartily and why she had apparently put on so much weight. Johnny Skinner was delighted and excited to think that, before long, his pig ... Penny's pig ... their pig, would give birth to a litter of piglets.

And how many would she have, he wondered. He knew that sometimes pigs can have as many as twelve or even more babies at one birth, but he knew also that a young sow like Lollipop would not have so many in her first litter.

And what colour would they be, he thought. He knew – because the Conjuror had told the King, who had told him – that the father of those unborn piglets was a very handsome coal-black boar.

Halfway through the month of June, Johnny was getting rather impatient for the answers to his questions.

King Theophilus also was very excited. How marvellous it would be if the pig actually had her babies on Penelope's birthday! What a wonderful day that would make it for the Princess! Nothing must spoil it, he thought. Then he suddenly thought that there was one person who might spoil it and that was his wife, who knew nothing of the secret and might object very strongly to the Palace being full of pigs.

I'll see if Cob can fix it, he said to himself. Eth thinks the world of that fellow since he cured her roses of black spot with that mixture of bird droppings and slug slime and mashed mouse manure.

"Don't worry yourself," the Conjuror said to the King. "I will have a word with Her Majesty, pointing out that Lollipop and however many babies she may have will be downstairs and close to the pig-flap and thus to the rose-garden, where in due course Queen Ethelwynne will have not just one pig to cultivate and manure her rose-beds, but lots."

"She's sure to be niggled," said the King, "because – apart from Penelope – she's the last to be told the secret."

"With your permission, sir," said the Conjuror, "I shall tell a little white lie. I shall tell the Queen that she is the first to be told. That ought to please her."

So he did,  and it did!

On the evening of June the twenty-second, the Queen's under-gardener went to sleep in his little cottage, hoping very much that Lollipop would give birth the following day. Johnny had been to say good night to her in her room and had seen that she was restless, moving the layers of horse-blankets about with her snout, as though trying to make some sort of bed.

He woke early next morning and dressed and crossed the garden. He ducked in through the new big pig-flap and stood in the passage outside Lollipop's room and listened.

To his great delight Johnny could hear a lot of little grunts and squeaks.

"Oh, Collie, you fixed it!" he said softly.

"No, no," said a voice behind him, and there stood the Conjuror in his many-coloured clothes. In his hand was his tall brimless top hat, which he'd taken off to get through the pig-flap. He put it back on his head.

"No," he said again. "It was nothing to do with me,

Johnny, how could it have been? Lady Lollipop just decided that she would have her babies on Penny's ninth birthday. A pure coincidence."

Johnny grinned.

"Wait till she sees them!" he said.

In fact they did not have to wait long, for in a few moments the Princess came running down the stairs and along the passage.

"Happy birthday, Penny!" said Johnny and the Conjuror with one voice.

"Oh, thank you!" said the Princess. "I'm just going to say good morning to my pig."

"*Our* pig," said Johnny.

Your pig*s*, thought the Conjuror.

At that instant, the Princess also heard the chorus of noise in Lollipop's room.

She dashed in. There, on a great nest of horse-blankets, lay Lady Lollipop, nursing her newborn piglets.

"Oh, how wonderful!" cried Princess Penelope. "Oh, Lollipop, how clever you are! Oh, what beautiful babies – some black, some white, some spotty! Oh, Johnny! Oh, Collie!"

The Princess lost no time in telling the news to her parents, and soon King Theophilus and Queen Ethelwynne arrived in their dressing-gowns, the King's nightcap still on his head.

"Oh, Lollipop!" cried the Queen. "What a clever girl you are!"

She turned to her husband.

"I was the first to be told the secret," she said. "You didn't know, Theo, did you?"

"Of course not, Eth," said the King.

He turned to his daughter.

"How many babies has she?" he asked.

"Well, Daddy," replied the Princess, "she has three white ones, two black ones and four spotty ones, and you know what three plus two plus four make, don't you?"

"Of course," said the King. "Um, er, let me see..."

"Nine!" cried the Princess.

"What a lovely surprise!"

CHAPTER THIRTEEN

When the grown-ups had gone, the King and Queen to get dressed for breakfast (to which they had invited the Conjuror), Princess Penelope and Johnny Skinner stood side by side, watching Lollipop suckling her babies.

"Oh, Duke," said the Princess. "What a lovely surprise! To think – I never knew! And she's had them on my birthday! And she's had nine, one for each year of my life! However did it happen?"

"Magic, I dare say," replied Johnny. "Mind you, she's clever, your pig is."

"*Our* pig," said the Princess. "Just think, we've got ten pigs now, Duke."

She looked at her friend.

"Daddy still hasn't remembered to make you one," she said.

"Doesn't worry me, Penny," said Johnny. "I'm quite happy just for you to call me that. By the way, the Conjuror told me that your father said he'd make him Sir Collie Cob."

"He'll forget," said the Princess. "Anyway, I think Lollipop's the one who really deserves to be honoured. No good asking Daddy. We'll do it, you and me. What shall we call her?"

Johnny looked fondly at the pig that had once been his and now was theirs, that had once been skinny and now was beautifully plump.

"She doesn't need another title," he said. "Let's just call her **clever Lollipop**!"